# TALES FROM CHINA

# OUTLAWS of the MARSH

D1073726

Vol.
01

# OUTLAWS of the MARSH

**Vol. 01**

## Spirits and Bandits

### Created by WEI DONG CHEN

*Wei Dong Chen is a highly acclaimed artist and an influential leader
in the "New Chinese Cartoon" trend. He is the founder of Creator World,
the largest comics studio in China. His spirited and energetic work has attracted
many students to his tutelage. He has published more than 300 cartoons in
several countries and gained both recognition and admirers across Asia, Europe,
and the USA. Mr. Chen's work is serialized in several publications,
and he continues to explore new dimensions of the graphic medium.*

### Illustrated by XIAO LONG LIANG

*Xiao Long Liang is considered one of Wei Dong Chen's greatest students.
One of the most highly regarded cartoonists in China today, Xiao Long's
fantastic technique and expression of Chinese culture have won him
the acclaim of cartoon lovers throughout China.*

**Original Story**
**"The Water Margin"** by Shi, Nai An

**Editing & Designing**
Jonathan Evans, KH Lee, YK Kim, HJ Lee,
JS Kim, Lampin, Qing Shao, Xiao Nan Li, Ke Hu

# Characters

## JIN WANG

Jin Wang is a martial arts master, and the former grand marshal of the royal imperial army of the Song Dynasty. When an old foe, Qiu Gao, chases Jin Wang and his mother from the capital, the two must trudge through the countryside looking for shelter. This will lead Jin Wang to meet a very auspicious young man with plenty of raw talent.

## QIU GAO

Qiu Gao rose from a background of desperate poverty to become, by way of ruthless scheming, the highest grand marshal under Emperor HuiZong of the Song Dynasty. Once he is installed, Qiu Gao seeks revenge against old rivals, including Jin Wang.

## LORD SHI

Lord Shi is a generous old man whose family owns a home on the outskirts of HuaYin Prefecture. One day he invites two travelers into his home, not knowing that one of them will alter the course of his son's life.

## JIN SHI

Jin Shi is a prodigious young man with an abundance of raw talent in martial arts. He is known as Nine Dragons, because of the tattoos on his body. When Jin Wang meets the young man, he instantly sees his potential, and asks to take Jin Shi as a student. The months they spend training together will turn Jin Shi into one of the great martial arts masters of his lifetime.

# Characters

## WU ZHU, DA CHEN, AND CHUN YANG

Wu Zhu, Da Chen, and Chun Yang are three low-level bandits who have run afoul of a local governor and have a bounty on their heads. They hatch a plot to kill the governor, a plot that requires them to cross paths with Jin Shi. When they do, they will learn the true extent, or limits, of their abilities.

## MAJOR DA LU (ZHISHEN LU)

Major Da Lu is a junior officer in a local village militia who has enormous appetites and an uncontrollable temper. When that temper gets him into trouble with the law, he must flee his village and seek shelter in a Buddhist temple. But even though his head is shaved and he's given the Buddhist name of ZhiShen, his true nature is no match for the quiet life of the monastery, and it doesn't take him long to find more trouble.

## ELDER PRIEST ZHIZHEN

ZhiZhen is the elder priest of WenShu Temple on Mount WuTai. Because of the temple's long relationship with the family of Lord Zhao, ZhiZhen agrees to shelter the fugitive Da Lu for a period of time. But he will soon learn that his charity endangers every monk in his temple.

## LORD LIU

Lord Liu is the master of Peach Blossom Manor. His daughter is set to be married, practically by force, to a local bandit. But when Lord Liu invites a traveling monk named ZhiShen Lu into his home, he doesn't realize that the wedding plans are about to be turned upside down.

## TONG ZHOU

Tong Zhou is a bandit who dwells on Mount Peach Blossom. He is set to marry Lord Liu's daughter in an arranged wedding, but Lord Liu has an unexpected guest who is willing to persuade Tong Zhou, by any means necessary, to call off the wedding.

# Chapter 1

# *Spirits and Bandits*

## Summary

During the reign of RenZong, fourth emperor of the Song Dynasty, a devastating epidemic ravaged the land. In an attempt to appease the gods and bring relief to his kingdom, RenZong instructed a grand marshal named Xin Hong to make an offering to the heavens. While doing so, Xin Hong came upon a strange vault with mysterious markings. According to legend, when Xin Hong opened the door, he unleashed more than 100 demons – 36 spirits and 72 fiends. These demons sought to create mischief and mayhem for the Song Dynasty.

Years later, during the reign of HuiZong, the eighth emperor of the Song Dynasty, a vicious schemer named Qiu Gao curried favor with the emperor and was installed as Supreme Grand Marshal of the Dynasty. Qiu Gao used his position to take revenge against an old adversary, Jin Wang, who had been Grand Marshal of the Imperial Guard. Jin Wang, along with his mother, fled the kingdom.

Jin Wang and his mother are bound for an area called YanAn when Jin Wang meets a young prodigy named Jin Shi. Wang takes the boy under his wing and trains him in the art of defense and attack. Soon after, Jin Shi becomes a master martial artist. Wang leaves when their training is complete, and some time later Jin Shi sets out to find his former master. Along the way, Jin Shi encounters a man with enormous strength, insatiable appetites, and a short-fuse temper that does as much harm as good. That man's name is Major Da Lu.

**Map of Modern China**

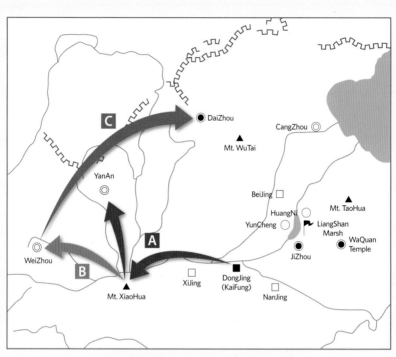

**Map of China During the Song Dynasty**

**A** Jin Wang and his mother are bound for YanAn when they encounter Jin Shi, commonly known as Nine Dragons. Jin Wang tutors him in martial arts, and leaves at the completion of his training.

**B** Some time later, Jin Shi sets out to find Jin Wang. In the town of WeiZhou, he meets Major Da Lu.

**C** After committing a heinous crime, Da Lu flees to DaiZhou.

In the days of the Song Dynasty, Grand Marshal Xin Hong was ordered by the emperor to ask for a heavenly blessing over the dynasty. While doing so, Xin Hong came upon the door to a mysterious vault. The inscription on the door said that the contents of the vault would remedy the ills of the one man who could open it – and the inscription said that man's name was Hong.

THERE...THERE'S NOTHING TO BE AFRAID OF. THE MARKINGS ON THE STONE SAY THAT ONLY I CAN OPEN IT. THAT MUST MEAN A HEAVENLY BLESSING CAN BE FOUND INSIDE!

OF COURSE... OF COURSE THAT'S WHAT IT SAYS. AND SURELY THE BEST DAYS OF YOUR KINGDOM ARE TO COME ONCE YOU OPEN THE SEAL.

THAT'S IT! YOU WANT TO OPEN IT

108 SPIRITS AND FIENDS, FREE AT LAST! NOW WE WILL DWELL IN PALACES AND MARSHES!

NO, THE SAME DREAM. THE ONE ABOUT QIU GAO.

In a wooded area far from the emperor's palace, Jin Wang, former grand marshal of the royal imperial military, was hiding out, along with his mother. The two had been driven out of the capital after the promotion of a man named Qiu Gao.

JIN, WAKE UP! WAKE UP, MY BOY! WHAT'S THE MATTER? ANOTHER DREAM?

EVERY NIGHT, THAT FIEND HAUNTS MY SLEEP. HE HAD ALWAYS RESENTED ME, I ASSUMED BECAUSE HE STARTED OUT AS NOTHING MORE THAN A STREET BUM. BUT IT'S WORSE THAN THAT.

NO SOONER HAD HE WEASELED HIS WAY INTO POWER THAN HE ACTUALLY TRIED TO KILL US. THAT MAN HAS A CORE OF PURE EVIL.

A SHORT TIME LATER, JIN WANG AND HIS MOTHER CAME TO A MANOR.

YOU'RE EXHAUSTED. LET'S SEE IF ANYONE'S HOME.

KNOCK KNOCK

HANG ON...

MOTHER, *LOOK!* DO YOU SEE THE LIGHTS OVER THERE?

I'M SORRY TO BOTHER YOU THIS LATE, BUT MY MOTHER AND I NEED A PLACE TO SLEEP.

≋ YAWN ≋ CAN I HELP YOU?

IF IT'S TOO MUCH TO ASK, I UNDERSTAND. WE CAN FIND LODGING ELSEWHERE.

WAIT JUST A MOMENT. I'LL FETCH MY MASTER.

THESE DAYS, PEOPLE MUST BAND TOGETHER IN ORDER TO SURVIVE. NOW, IF YOU'LL WAIT JUST A FEW MORE MINUTES, I'LL HAVE MY MEN PREPARE YOUR ROOM. WOULD YOU, PLEASE?

YES, MY LORD.

Early the next morning…

CHIRP CHIRP

THMP

MOTHER? *MOTHER!*

MOTHER, WHAT'S WRONG? TALK TO ME! I CAN'T HELP YOU UNLESS I KNOW WHAT'S HAPPENING.

YOUNG MAN, I'M COMING IN. WHAT'S WRONG?

KREAK

OUR JOURNEY HAS TAKEN A TOLL. SHE'S TOO OLD FOR THIS.

SHE HAS A HIGH FEVER AND EXHAUSTION.

WELL, IT IS CLEAR THAT YOU TWO CAN'T LEAVE RIGHT AWAY. YOU MUST STAY UNTIL SHE'S BETTER.

Jin Wang and his mother stayed at the manor for several more days while she recovered.

AGAIN, I THANK YOU.

One day, while Jin Wang was wandering around the manor…

So Jin Shi became Jin Wang's student, and they trained night and day for six months. During this time, Jin Shi became a master of 18 different weapons.

By the end of that time, Jin Shi was an expert martial artist, and Jin Wang decided to travel with his mother to YanAn, as they had originally planned.

BUT I DON'T UNDERSTAND. WHY ARE YOU LEAVING NOW, WHEN I HAVE SO MUCH LEFT TO LEARN?

HAVE WE NOT TAKEN GOOD CARE OF YOU? WE'LL KEEP DOING IT, I PROMISE.

IT'S NOT THAT. QIU GAO IS CHASING US.

THE LONGER I STAY, THE MORE I PUT YOU AT RISK.

SETTLE DOWN, SON.

I'D LIKE TO THANK YOU FOR ALL YOU'VE DONE FOR US. I'M SORRY TO BE LEAVING THIS PLACE.

AND WE'RE SORRY TO SEE YOU GO.

BEFORE YOU LEAVE, PLEASE TAKE THESE. THEY ARE SILVER PIECES THAT CAN BE USED AS CURRENCY.

DON'T WORRY, JIN SHI. I HAVE TAUGHT YOU EVERYTHING I KNOW. AND IF YOU CONTINUE PERFECTING YOUR MIND AND BODY EVERY DAY, I PROMISE YOU WILL DO GREAT THINGS.

I DON'T KNOW WHAT TO SAY, EXCEPT THANK YOU AGAIN.

ALL RIGHT, JIN SHI. THAT'S FAR ENOUGH.

FAREWELL, MY LORD.

TAKE CARE OF YOURSELF.

FAREWELL. WE WILL MEET AGAIN SOMEDAY.

GOODBYE, MASTER. I HOPE YOU ARE RIGHT.

UNTIL THAT DAY, I PLEDGE TO PRACTICE WHAT YOU TAUGHT ME.

JIN SHI WAS AS GOOD AS HIS WORD. HE PRACTICED DAY AND NIGHT, WEEK AFTER WEEK.

AND SURE ENOUGH, HE GOT EVEN BETTER.

ONE DAY, A BAND OF THREE THIEVES--WU ZHU, DA CHEN, AND CHUN YANG-- TOOK SHELTER IN A MANOR NEAR THE SHI RESIDENCE. THEIR ARRIVAL WOULD CHANGE JIN SHI'S LIFE FOREVER.

CHUN YANG

DA CHEN

WU ZHU

WE'VE ALL HEARD MYTHS ABOUT JIN SHI. BUT HE'S JUST A BOY!

LET ME AT HIM! WE'LL PASS THROUGH THESE LANDS WITHOUT ISSUE.

I'LL BE BACK IN NO LESS THAN AN HOUR. AND I'LL BRING HIS HEAD BACK WITH ME.

WAIT! DON'T--

HYAH!

43

DA CHEN, I HEREBY FORGIVE YOUR AGGRESSIVE ACTS. YOU MAY LEAVE WITH YOUR BROTHERS NOW.

THANK YOU, MY LORD.

IT IS AN HONOR TO BOW BEFORE YOU.

ALL HAIL!

PLEASE, GET OFF THE FLOOR.

THE THREE OF YOU MOVED ME WITH YOUR INCREDIBLE SHOW OF FIDELITY.

WHAT DO YOU SAY WE HAVE DRINK TOGETHER? OR SIX?

WHAT'S MINE IS YOURS.

WE ACCEPT, ON THE CONDITION THAT WE MAY CALL YOU MASTER!

Thus Jin Shi became good friends with the three bandits.

The bandits returned to their manor, and they remained good friends with Jin Shi. On the occasion of the Moon Festival, Jin Shi dispatched a messenger to deliver an invitation to the three men. Before he returned with their reply, the messenger got very drunk.

NOTE TO SELF: NO MORE DRUNK DELIVERY.

FMP

WHOO... THAT LAST DRINK WAS A KICKER.

OOF!

FWOMP

ON YOUR FEET! WAKE UP!

GREAT. ANOTHER NIGHT, ANOTHER MESSENGER I GET TO CARRY HOME.

≋ BRRP ≋

HMAWHA?

YOU PASSED OUT DRUNK. AGAIN.

AND THIS TIME, YOU APPEAR TO BE CARRYING A LOT OF MONEY.

OH, AND A LETTER. I WONDER...

I DON'T BELIEVE IT!

ACCORDING TO THIS, MASTER JIN SHI'S THREE FRIENDS ARE NOTHING MORE THAN A BAND OF THIEVES. AND NOT JUST ANY THIEVES-- THIEVES WITH AN ENORMOUS BOUNTY ON THEIR HEADS!

LOOKS LIKE THE HEAVENS ARE ON MY SIDE TODAY!

I HAVE TO GET TO THE GOVERNOR'S OFFICE RIGHT AWAY. THIS IS THE PAYDAY I'VE BEEN WAITING FOR!

A few weeks later, it was time for the Moon Festival, and the three bandit captains set out for Jin Shi's manor bearing gifts.

ALL RIGHT, YOU GUYS KNOW THE DRILL. TAKE THE BANDITS DOWN. NO SURVIVORS.

THE POLICE ARE HERE FOR YOU. WHY IS THAT?

WHAT THE...?

WELL, YOU SEE, MASTER... THERE MIGHT BE A PRICE ON OUR HEADS. BUT WE SWEAR WE NEVER MEANT TO CAUSE YOU HARM!

HA HA HA! MY FRIENDS, YOU AREN'T THE ONLY GOOD MEN IN THIS LAND WITH PRICES ON YOUR HEADS.

WAIT HERE. I WILL TAKE CARE OF THIS SITUATION.

GREETINGS, MY LORD. WHAT BRINGS YOU OUT IN SUCH NUMBERS AT THIS TIME OF NIGHT?

DON'T PRETEND LIKE YOU DON'T KNOW THE ANSWER TO THAT. AND DON'T TRY TO HIDE PREY FROM A PREDATOR!

WE HAVE A LETTER TO YOU BY THE BANDITS!

MIND YOUR TONGUE, MINION. WHAT MAKES YOU THINK YOU CAN TALK TO ME THAT WAY?

WHAT LETTER? YOU NEVER TOLD ME THERE WAS A LETTER SENT IN REPLY.

WELL...YOU SEE...I WAS A LITTLE DRUNK, AND--

SAVE IT. I'LL DEAL WITH YOU LATER. VERY WELL! I WILL COMPLY. TELL YOUR FORCES TO STAND DOWN, AND I WILL HAND THE BANDITS OVER TO YOU!

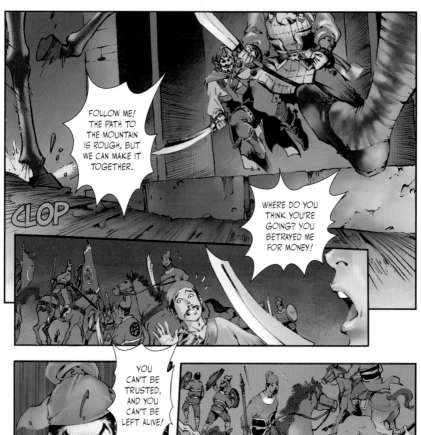

FOLLOW ME! THE PATH TO THE MOUNTAIN IS ROUGH, BUT WE CAN MAKE IT TOGETHER.

WHERE DO YOU THINK YOU'RE GOING? YOU BETRAYED ME FOR MONEY!

CLOP

YOU CAN'T BE TRUSTED, AND YOU CAN'T BE LEFT ALIVE!

MY LORD, PLEASE! SPARE MY LIFE! I ≶ GUHK ≶

NEVER MIND THE UNDERLINGS! I WANT THE HEAD OF THE HOUSE AND THE BANDITS!

Jin Shi and the three bandits narrowly escaped back to the mountain. But now Jin Shi was tormented about being a man without a home.

AS I AM NOW HOMELESS, I FIND IT DIFFICULT TO KNOW MY PLACE IN THE WORLD. I FEEL LIKE I DON'T BELONG ANYWHERE.

THAT BEING THE CASE, I SHALL SEEK OUT MY MASTER, JIN WANG.

WHAT ARE YOU TALKING ABOUT, MASTER? YOUR PLACE IS HERE, WITH US. LET US REPAY YOU THE GENEROSITY YOU SHOWED US.

Jin Shi had heard that Jin Wang was in JingLuo, so he set out on a path that would take him there by way of the city of WeiZhou.

FAREWELL, MASTER. TAKE GOOD CARE OF YOURSELF.

YOU, TOO. AND REST ASSURED: WE'LL MEET AGAIN SOMEDAY.

WEIZHOU

SPARE SOME CHANGE, MY LORD?

A CUP OF TEA, PLEASE.

PERHAPS YOU CAN HELP ME. I AM ON MY WAY TO JINGLUO, AND I'M LOOKING FOR A MAN NAMED JIN WANG. HAVE YOU HEARD OF HIM?

JIN WANG?

CAN'T SAY I HAVE, BUT THERE ARE A LOT OF MEN WITH THE LAST NAME OF WANG AROUND HERE.

THIS ONE WOULD STAND OUT. HE WAS ONCE THE GRAND MARSHAL OF THE IMPERIAL FORCES.

THMP

OH! THEN I BET MAJOR LU KNOWS HIM.

61

LET'S SEE... JIN WANG...HE WAS BEING CHASED BY QIU GAO, YES?

THEN I WOULD BET ALL THE MONEY I DON'T HAVE THAT HE'S IN YANAN, UNDER THE WATCHFUL EYE OF HU CHONG.

I KNOW THIS BECAUSE THIS TOWN IS GOVERNED BY HIS BROTHER, XIAO CHONG. THEY'RE BOTH GOOD MEN.

I'M AFRAID SO.

REST EASY, YOUNG MAN. YOUR MASTER IS IN SAFE HANDS. FOR NOW, YOU AND I HAVE DRINKING TO DO!

IT WOULD BE CRIMINAL TO NOT RAISE A GLASS TO A MARTIAL ARTS MASTER SUCH AS YOURSELF.

GOOD DAY, FRIENDS.

THEY'RE NOT HAVING THE BEST OF LUCK RIGHT NOW. FORGIVE THEM.

I'M SO SORRY ABOUT THE NOISE, MY LORD. I HAVE GUESTS IN THE BACK.

I DECIDE FOR MYSELF WHOM I FORGIVE! BRING THEM OUT HERE!

NOW YOU'VE DONE IT. MAJOR DA LU WANTS TO SEE YOU.

MY LORD. IT'S AN HONOR TO MEET YOU.

SAVE IT. WHAT'S THE PROBLEM? IF IT TURNS OUT TO BE NOTHING, I'LL THUMP YOUR SKULL.

MY NAME IS JIN. THIS IS MY DAUGHTER, CUILIAN. WE ARE FROM JINGCHENG. WE CAME HERE TO LIVE WITH RELATIVES, BUT WHEN WE ARRIVED, THEY WERE GONE. WE HAD TO LIVE ON THE STREETS. A SHORT TIME LATER, MY WIFE DIED.

ONE DAY, A MAN NAMED TUFU ZHENG SAW CUILIAN AND OFFERED A DOWRY SO HE COULD MAKE HER HIS OWN. I ACCEPTED BECAUSE WE WERE DESPERATE.

BUT WHEN THE TIME CAME FOR HIM TO PAY THE DOWRY, HE REFUSED.

WE DIDN'T THINK TOO MUCH OF IT, BECAUSE AT LEAST WE'D HAVE A PLACE TO LIVE. BUT ON THE DAY WE MOVED IN, WE LEARNED THE MAN WAS ALREADY MARRIED, AND HIS WIFE DESPISED US.

SO WE WERE KICKED OUT, BACK ON THE STREETS, AND ORDERED TO REPAY MONEY WE WERE NEVER PAID TO BEGIN WITH! AND HE THREATENED TO TRULY HURT US IF I DON'T COME UP WITH THE MONEY.

BUT HE NEVER GAVE US THE MONEY, SO HOW DO I COME UP WITH IT? MY DAUGHTER IS HYSTERICAL WITH ANXIETY, AND I HAVE LOST HOPE.

DEEPEST APOLOGIES, MY LORD. WE JUST DON'T KNOW WHAT TO DO. WE HAVE NOWHERE TO GO AND NO ONE TO TURN TO.

THAT'S IT! I'VE HEARD MORE THAN ENOUGH! YOU SAID THIS BASTARD'S NAME WAS TUFU ZHENG?

YES, MY LORD. HE OWNS THE BUTCHER SHOP OVER NEAR JINLIANG BRIDGE. HE HAS A REPUTATION FOR BRUTALITY.

SLAM

OH, YEAH? WELL, THAT REPUTATION IS ABOUT TO TAKE A BEATING.

NOBODY BULLIES STRANGERS IN MY TOWN!

BY THE TIME I'M DONE, HE'LL HAVE A REPUTATION FOR BEING A PUNCHING BAG.

MAJOR, WAIT! YOU DON'T WANT TO STORM OUT THERE LIKE THIS. YOUR TEMPER COULD GET YOU IN TROUBLE.

The next morning…

KEEP AN EYE OUT. HE SAID HE'D BE HERE ANY MINUTE NOW.

?

HEY, LOOK WHO'S UP EARLY.

HELLO THERE, MY LADY. DON'T YOU LOOK LOVELY THIS MORNING.

ALL RIGHT, I'M HERE! READY TO GO?

WHAM

GAH!

BUT, BUT... MY LORD! TUFU ZHENG PUT ME IN CHARGE OF PATROLLING THIS MANOR. ONE OF MY JOBS IS TO MAKE SURE THESE TWO DON'T FLEE!

WELL, CONSIDER YOURSELF FIRED. I'LL DEAL WITH YOUR BOSS.

YOU DON'T GET IT! IF I LET THEM--

THAT'S ENOUGH! LET'S SEE YOU MOUTH OFF WITH NO TEETH!

THUMP

WHACK

HEY!

IT'S BEEN TWO HOURS. NOW TO SEE THE BUTCHER.

壯元橋

As requested, Zheng minced the leanest pork he had.

HERE WE GO. ALL DONE. SHALL I HAVE IT DELIVERED?

I'M NOT DONE!

I NEED 5 MORE POUNDS OF MINCED PORK. ONLY THIS TIME, I WANT THE FATTIEST STUFF.

FATTIEST...? WHY DO YOU NEED SO MUCH MEAT?

NONE OF YOUR BUSINESS! START MINCING.

VERY WELL. WHATEVER YOU SAY.

Major Da Lu continued to harass Zheng through the morning and into the afternoon.

IS THE BUTCHER SHOP OPEN?

IT IS. BUT MAJOR LU IS CAUSING SUCH A SCENE THAT NO ONE DARES GO IN.

ALL RIGHT. I'M FINISHED. TAKE IT TO HIM.

YOU'RE NOT DONE YET! NOW I NEED 5 POUNDS OF MINCED GRISTLE!

AND IF THERE'S ANY MEAT ON IT, THERE WILL BE HELL TO PAY.

Realizing he had gotten carried away and beaten the butcher to death, Da Lu immediately fled WeiZhou. He knew the authorities would soon be after him, so he kept off the main roads and traveled through heavily wooded areas.

FINALLY. A TOWN. I NEED TO SEE IF NEWS OF THE BUTCHER HAS TRAVELED.

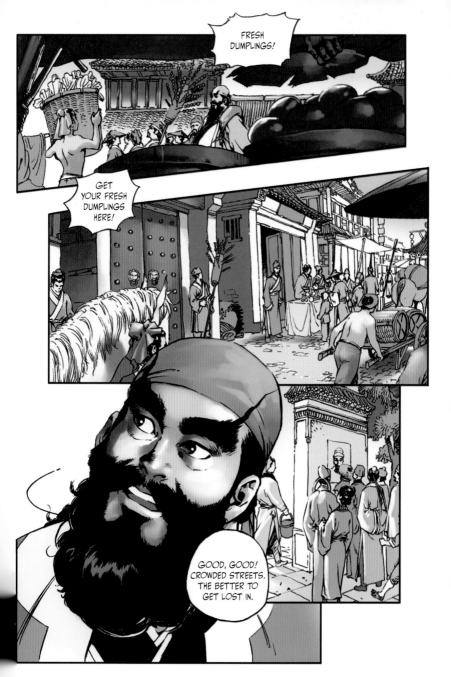

# Chapter 2

# *The Stubborn Violence of Lu*

## Summary

Having fled WeiZhou, Da Lu reaches DaiZhou. Da Lu goes to the town square, where he learns he's wanted for murder, when he reunites with Old Man Jin and his daughter, CuiLian. They remain indebted to Da Lu for freeing them from the butcher, and hide him in the home of Lord Zhao, who is CuiLian's new husband. Soon, though, the authorities become aware of Da Lu's presence, and Lord Zhao sends Da Lu to a Buddhist temple, where the authorities would never look for a criminal.

Da Lu a arrives at the Buddhist temple, and immediately his head is shaved and he is given the Buddhist name ZhiShen. But looks and name alone do not make one a Buddhist priest, and soon Lu's true nature shines through in ways that threaten his safety, and the safety of everyone around him.

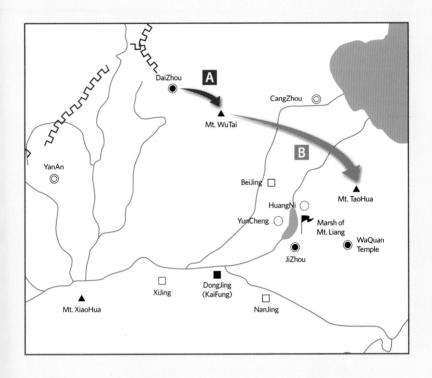

**A** With the help of Lord Zhao, Da Lu goes to join the monks of WenShu Temple on Mount WuTai. Da Lu is renamed ZhiShen Lu.

**B** ZhiShen Lu wears out his welcome on Mount WuTai, and is sent to live in a temple in DongJing. Along the way, he spends a night in Lord Liu's Peach Blossom (TaoHua) Manor.

HAHAHA!

FALSE ALARM. IT'S NOT A BANDIT. IT'S A MOST IMPORTANT GUEST.

MAJOR DA LU. IT IS AN HONOR TO FINALLY MEET YOU.

AND WHO ARE YOU?

THIS IS THE MAN I TOLD YOU ABOUT, LORD ZHAO.

HE CAME HOME AND THOUGHT A THIEF HAD BROKEN IN AND MEANT TO HARM US.

99

**The House of Grass**

MY LORD! MAJOR DA LU!!

Major Da Lu had expected to stay as a guest of the manor until things calmed down. But before too long…

OLD MAN JIN, WHAT'S WRONG? WHY ARE YOU OUT OF BREATH?

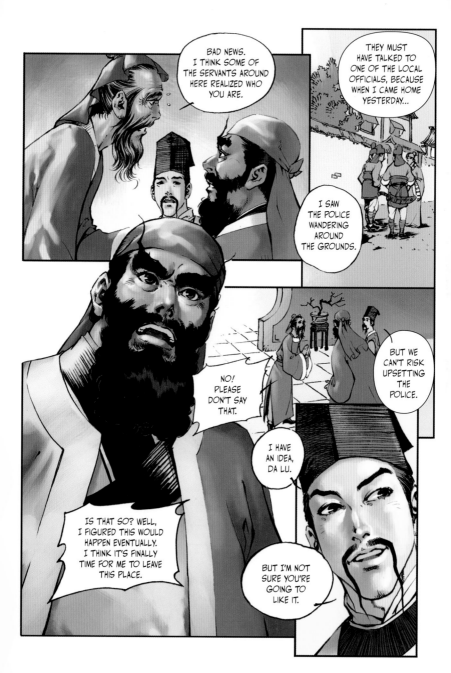

BAD NEWS. I THINK SOME OF THE SERVANTS AROUND HERE REALIZED WHO YOU ARE.

THEY MUST HAVE TALKED TO ONE OF THE LOCAL OFFICIALS, BECAUSE WHEN I CAME HOME YESTERDAY...

I SAW THE POLICE WANDERING AROUND THE GROUNDS.

BUT WE CAN'T RISK UPSETTING THE POLICE.

NO! PLEASE DON'T SAY THAT.

I HAVE AN IDEA, DA LU.

IS THAT SO? WELL, I FIGURED THIS WOULD HAPPEN EVENTUALLY. I THINK IT'S FINALLY TIME FOR ME TO LEAVE THIS PLACE.

BUT I'M NOT SURE YOU'RE GOING TO LIKE IT.

THERE IS A BUDDHIST TEMPLE ON MOUNT WUTAI CALLED WENSHU. I KNOW IT WELL.

YOU GOTTA BE KIDDING. A TEMPLE? NOT IN A MILLION--OH, WHO AM I KIDDING? I HAVE NO CHOICE.

MY FAMILY HAS TITHED AT THE TEMPLE FOR GENERATIONS.

ALL RIGHT, I'LL GO! BUT I'LL TELL YOU RIGHT NOW I'M NOT EXACTLY BUDDHIST PRIEST MATERIAL.

IF I ASK, I'M SURE THEY'LL LET YOU STAY WITH THEM.

THE AUTHORITIES WOULD NEVER THINK TO LOOK THERE.

The next morning...

WenShu temple agreed to shelter Da Lu, but the chief priest, ZhiZhen, was wary of Da Lu's sharp eyes and murderous look. So he set forth a few rules.

YOU'RE NUTS IF YOU THINK I'M SHAVING MY HEAD.

SHINK SHUNK

HEY! WHAT ARE YOU--

NOW LISTEN, ZHISHEN...

UM, OKAY...

HERE, WE LIVE BY THE FIVE BUDDHIST COMMANDMENTS. THEY PROHIBIT THE FOLLOWING...

So Major Da Lu became the Buddhist monk ZhiShen, but the transition was only skin deep. ZhiShen soon became impatient with monastic life, and even grew bitter toward Lord Zhao, who'd saved his life. Three short months later...

MURDER, THEFT, ADULTERY, LYING, AND INTEMPERANCE.

TO VIOLATE ONE OF THESE IS TO FORFEIT YOUR LIFE.

OH, JUST SOME WINE I MADE EARLIER THIS WEEK.

HI, THERE. WHAT'S THAT YOU'RE CARRYING?

OH, YEAH? HOW MUCH FOR IT?

HA! WAIT, ARE YOU BEING SERIOUS?

I'M BEING SERIOUS.

BUT... BUDDHIST MONKS AREN'T ALLOWED TO DRINK! I SHOULD KNOW. I LIVE NEXT TO THE TEMPLE.

IF WORD GOT OUT THAT I'D SOLD WINE TO A MONK, I'D BE IN BIG TROUBLE. MY FAMILY WOULD KILL ME.

LOOK, YOU LITTLE WIMP. SELL ME THE WINE, OR I'LL KILL YOU MYSELF.

ZhiShen then proceeded to drink the entire barrel right in front of the man.

114

115

FOOMP

GAK!

ZHISHEN, STOP!!! THIS IS NO WAY TO ACT IN A HOUSE OF WORSHIP!

EVERYONE PUT YOUR ARMS DOWN!

PRIEST ZHIZHEN IS HERE!

The next morning, ZhiShen was truly sorry for the trouble he'd caused.

TELL ME: DO YOU STILL THINK YOU'RE LIVING IN THE OUTSIDE WORLD?

DO YOU STILL THINK YOU CAN GET DRUNK AND BEAT PEOPLE BECAUSE IT AMUSES YOU?

COME IN, ZHISHEN.

YOU ARE HERE BECAUSE THAT BEHAVIOR GOT YOU IN TROUBLE. AND YOU KNOW FULL WELL OUR RULES ABOUT FIGHTING AND ALCOHOL.

I'M SORRY, I REALLY AM. IT WON'T HAPPEN AGAIN.

FWMP

123

WELL I LIKE IT A LOT. MORE LIQUOR!

BROTHER, YOU'RE GOING TO PUT ME OUT OF BUSINESS.

THIS IS GOING TO RUIN MY REPUTATION.

BUUURRRRRPPP

AHEM. EXCUSE ME.

FINE. I'M GOING. THANKS FOR THE MEAT AND BOOZE.

127

HE'S COMPLETELY DRUNK AGAIN AND ACTING LIKE SOME KIND OF CAGED ANIMAL. HE JUST DESTROYED JINGANG STATUE IN FRONT OF THE MAIN GATE.

PRIEST ZHIZHEN! COME QUICK!

IT'S ZHISHEN!

WHAT IS IT NOW?

UNDERSTOOD. STAY AWAY FROM HIM, AND GO ABOUT YOUR BUSINESS.

BUT THAT STATUE WAS SACRED! WE CAN'T JUST TURN OUR BACKS--

ZHISHEN COULD DESTROY THIS WHOLE TEMPLE, AND IT WOULDN'T MAKE US ANY LESS FAITHFUL STUDENTS OF BUDDHA. REMEMBER, BUDDHA LIVES IN OUR HEARTS, NOT IN THE STONE OF SOME STATUE; IT CAN'T BE SMASHED TO BITS. THE TRUE NATURE OF BUDDHA IS IN YOUR HEART.

A STATUE IS NOTHING MORE THAN A TOKEN OF TRUE FAITH.

BESIDES, LORD ZHAO WILL BUILD A NEW STATUE FOR US. SO WE'VE LOST NOTHING.

NOW GO ABOUT YOUR DAYS. I'LL DEAL WITH THIS.

WHAM!

AH-HA!

ALL RIGHT! WHO'S READY TO JOIN THEIR DEPARTED ANCESTORS?!

HOLD YOUR GROUND, BROTHERS! WE MUST DRIVE HIM OUT.

HOLD...

147

ACK!

WHOMP

149

The next morning…

ZHISHEN, I'M SURE YOU UNDERSTAND THAT IT IS TIME FOR YOU TO LEAVE THIS PLACE. I KNOW OF ANOTHER TEMPLE IN JINGCHENG. YOU CAN STAY THERE.

BUT I WANT TO SEND YOU WITH MORE THAN JUST A LETTER. I WANT TO ARM YOU WITH FOUR BUDDHIST PHRASES. PHRASES YOU CAN KEEP WITH YOU AND SPEAK FOR THE REST OF YOUR LIFE.

"WHEN YOU SEE A FOREST, LIFE WILL GET BETTER. WHEN YOU SEE A MOUNTAIN, YOU WILL GET RICH. WHEN YOU COME TO A VILLAGE, MOVE ON. WHEN YOU COME TO A RIVER, STOP."

BUDDHIST PHRASES?

I WILL SEND YOU OUT WITH A PERSONAL LETTER FROM ME. THAT SHOULD SMOOTH THINGS OVER FOR YOU WHEN YOU ARRIVE.

HUH?

THANK YOU FOR ALL YOU'VE DONE FOR ME. I WON'T FORGET IT.

SAVE US, MERCIFUL BUDDHA...

HM.

YOU KNOW, SOMEDAY I REALLY SHOULD COME BACK HERE AND FIX THAT GATE...

ZhiShen walked down Mount WuTai, collected the sword and staff he had ordered, and set out for JingCheng.

ZhiShen knew that he was still wanted by the authorities, so he pressed on, walking day and night until he reached his destination.

155

157

MY LORD, THIS LOWLY MONK BARGED IN, AND NOW HE'S TRYING TO PICK A FIGHT.

HMPH...

MY SONS MAY NOT RESPECT A MAN OF FAITH, BUT THEIR OLD MAN IS A TRUE BUDDHIST.

UNFORTUNATELY, WE'RE HAVING SOME FAMILY ISSUES AT THE MOMENT.

I DIDN'T WANT TO! MY LORD, I AM TRAVELING FROM WUTAI TO JINGCHENG, AND I WAS LOOKING FOR A PLACE TO SLEEP. THIS GUY RESPONDED BY THREATENING TO LOCK ME IN THE SHED.

YOU ARE FROM MOUNT WUTAI? WELL, THEN! PLEASE COME IN.

I'M AFRAID ONE NIGHT IS ALL YOU CAN STAY.

AND HAVE AS MUCH WINE AS YOU LIKE. IT WILL HELP YOU SLEEP THROUGH THE NOISE TONIGHT.

I DON'T MEAN TO CAUSE ANY MORE TROUBLE FOR YOUR FAMILY. I CAN LEAVE, IF IT WOULD MAKE THINGS EASIER.

OH, NO. IT HAS NOTHING TO DO WITH YOU. IT'S MY DAUGHTER. SHE'S GETTING MARRIED TONIGHT AND, WELL, I HAVE SOME CONCERNS.

NOISE? WHAT'S GOING ON?

*HA HA!* IS THAT ALL? THAT'S NOTHING TO WORRY ABOUT. IT'S NATURAL FOR A FATHER TO WORRY ON THE DAY HIS DAUGHTER GETS MARRIED.

NO. THIS IS AN ARRANGED MARRIAGE. ONE I DON'T WANT.

YOU SEE, THERE ARE TWO BANDITS WHO DWELL IN THE NEARBY MOUNTAINS. THEY ARE SO POWERFUL AND SO FEARED THAT EVEN THE LOCAL GOVERNMENT CAN'T CONTROL THEM.

ONE OF THEM HAS HAD EYES FOR MY DAUGHTER SINCE THE DAY HE ARRIVED.

I DIDN'T CONSENT TO THE MARRIAGE BECAUSE I WAS GIVEN NO CHOICE. HENCE MY REMORSE.

TONG ZHOU

THUD

As was tradition, father and son sat together for many rounds of drinking.

TELL ME... ≷ BRRP ≷ WHERE IS THE BRIDE TO BE?

OH, SHE'S TOO SHY TO BE SEEN.

FAIR ENOUGH. ANOTHER ROUND THEN! I HAVE TO CELEBRATE THIS MARRIAGE WITH SOMEONE, SO WHY NOT YOU?

KLINK

AH... I'D LIKE TO SEE MY WIFE NOW.

HERE WE ARE. SHE'S RIGHT THROUGH HERE.

GULP GULP

OF COURSE. LET ME SHOW YOU TO THE BRIDAL SUITE.

GOOD NIGHT, SON.

*HMPH.* MY FATHER-IN-LAW IS A CHEAPSKATE. WON'T SPEND FOR ENOUGH OIL TO KEEP THE LAMPS LIT.

SOMEONE BRING ME SOME OIL! IT'S MY WEDDING NIGHT!

*HEH HEH.* SURE IS. A NIGHT YOU'RE GOING TO REMEMBER FOR THE REST OF YOUR LIFE.

MY DARLING, ARE YOU IN HERE? YOUR HUSBAND WOULD HAVE SOME BUSINESS WITH YOU.

WHAT'S THE MATTER? TOO SHY TO LIGHT A CANDLE?

# *Once Upon a Time in a Lawless Land...*

*Outlaws of the Marsh,* also known as *Water Margin*, is one of the four great works of Chinese literature. Like its companions in the Eastern canon – *Journey to the West, Romance of the Three Kingdoms,* and *Dream of the Red Chamber* – *Outlaws* is a story that has been told many ways over the centuries. And like those other three stories, *Outlaws* contains many story elements and themes that would be familiar to a Western reader who loves stories of cowboys, bandits, or gangsters.

When the story opens, China is under the rule of the Song Dynasty. It is immediately clear that the dynasty is weak; the emperor keeps himself hidden away, and responds to real-world problems by making offerings to the heavens rather than finding solutions. He has allowed Grand Marshal Qiu Gao, a scheming and vindictive man, to wield power without oversight. As a result, the Song Dynasty is controlled by a tyrant whose influence is far-reaching, but who is so preoccupied with his own agenda that he does a poor job of maintaining law and order throughout the land. This means that there are vast stretches of China where crime, corruption, and lawlessness are a normal part of everyday life. And much like the cowboys of the old west, the people who live in these areas have little respect for authority and rely on themselves for protection and order.

The results of this vary widely. A man like Major Da Lu is a volatile and violent man who intimidates everyone around him and acts as judge, jury, and executioner. On the other hand, a man like Jin Shi is instilled with a code of conduct and honor by his father, which balances out the lethal skills he learns from the exiled Marshal Jin Wang. Both of these men are capable of killing with ruthless efficiency, but only one has the maturity to balance that impulse with wisdom. Neither man wishes to answer to an authority greater than himself, but where Jin Shi handles himself with finesse, Da Lu handles himself like a raging bull.

Of course, despite the lawlessness, there do exist actual laws, and when Da Lu kills a man in cold blood, he must run for his life. While in hiding, Da Lu learns just how widespread the disorder truly is: tucked away in a monastery, tasked with the simple matter of behaving himself and living quietly until things calm down for him, Da Lu cannot help but get drunk and wreak havoc in the temple. This is a man on the wrong side of the law, but with so little comprehension of why laws and rules exist that he breaks them as casually as taking a breath. Major Da Lu is a product of the environment in which he lives, and he is proof that in such a lawless environment, chaos seeps into everything and everyone – and the true menace to social order may just be an individual acting in his own interests.

DA LU